Mary Malloy
and
The Baby Who Wouldn't Sleep

Written and illustrated by
- Niki Daly -

GOLDEN BOOKS
WESTERN PUBLISHING COMPANY, INC.

GOLDEN BOOKS
WESTERN PUBLISHING COMPANY, INC.
850 THIRD AVENUE, NEW YORK, NEW YORK 10022

Library of Congress Cataloging-in-Publication Data
Daly, Niki.
Mary Malloy and the baby who wouldn't sleep /
written and illustrated by Niki Daly
p.   cm.
Summary: The sly seductive moon makes off with a crying baby
but is eventually outwitted by the clever Mr. Fez.
[1. Moon–Fiction. 2. Babies–Fiction.] I. Title.
PZ7.D1715Mar 1993
[E]–dc20   92-41884 CIP AC
ISBN 0-307-17501-4

For all the babies
I have rocked to sleep.

~ND~

Baby wouldn't go to sleep.

He cried, he hollered, he sobbed, he wailed.
He shook Mary Malloy right out of a dream.

Mary Malloy put on her hat and went to see Baby.
"What's wrong? Want a song?" whispered Mary.
"Boo-hoo-hoo!" cried Baby.

Mary Malloy carried Baby onto the verandah,
where the cool evening air stroked Baby's hot cheeks.

"Go to sleep, my Mama's cuckoo-lulu," sang Mary.
"Big Bear's gonna eat you up IF YOU DON'T!"

Baby hullabalooed until the Crescent Moon
pushed aside her cloudy curtains and smiled
mysteriously down at Mary Malloy and the
baby who wouldn't go to sleep.

"Babies love being rocked," cooed Moon. "Let me rock him."
"Only if you're very careful not to let him fall," said Mary Malloy,
placing Baby into Moon's waiting arms.

"Oooh," crooned Moon as Baby curled into her.
"I *do* love babies."

Full and round, Moon rocked Baby.
But Baby om-pom-pushed and boo-hooed
fit to wake the world.

"Moon," called out Mary Malloy,
"please don't hold Baby so tightly."

"Fiddlesticks!" chuckled the moon.

"Moon, give me back Baby!" demanded Mary Malloy.
"Tricked you!" laughed the wicked moon from behind
her spidery curtains.

Now Moon tried to soothe Baby.
She hushabyed and kootchie-cooed.
She sang velvety lullabies across the silver sea.

"MOON! YOU THIEF,
BRING BACK BABY!"
Mary Malloy's voice echoed
from the West to the East,
across the sea and over cities
that never sleep, all the way
to the distant Nile.

There,
Mr. Fez, the crocodile,
saw the moon above the Nile,
caught its wicked moonlight smile
laughing on the water.

So this is what he did.

"Moon," called Mr. Fez, "see what I have for you."
Moon looked down and eyed a beautiful water baby shining
in the water.

"Aaah," sighed Moon, "I *do* love babies. And two are better than
one!" Moon beamed over the water. The water baby grew big and
bonny as Moon dipped and danced closer and closer.

Foolishly, Moon opened her arms to snatch up
the water baby and as she did so – *splash!* – Baby fell
into the bubbly Nile, right into Mr. Fez's fishing net.
"Goo-goo," gurgled Baby. He had stopped crying.

"Tricked you, Moon!" laughed Mr. Fez.
Quickly, he fished Baby out of the warm water.

Mr. Fez placed Baby safely into his felucca,
and they floated bubbly, bubbly, down the Nile . . .

across the silver sea . . .

and before they reached journey's end,
Baby fell fast asleep.

"Thank you and good night," whispered Mary Malloy,
carrying Baby back to bed.

High above, the Crescent Moon hung thin and sullen.
A tear fell from her eye and turned into an evening star.
Moon smiled sadly and sighed, "At least I have you."

Mr. Fez gazed up at the sky and tenderly sang,
"Twinkle, twinkle, star so bright,
Shining in the pale moonlight,

"Kiss the baby, cheek and chin,
Bless the bed that I lie in.

"North, South, East, West,
Choose the dream that you love best."

Good night!